The Little Nut Tree

There are lots of Early Reader stories
you might enjoy.

Look at the back of the book or, for a complete list,
visit www.orionbooks.co.uk

The Little Nut Tree

Written and Illustrated by

Sally Gardner

Orion
Children's Books

The Little Nut Tree was originally published in 1993
by Orion Children's Books
This edition first published in Great Britain in 2014
by Orion Children's Books
a division of the Orion Publishing Group Ltd
Orion House
5 Upper Saint Martin's Lane
London WC2H 9EA
An Hachette UK Company

1 3 5 7 9 10 8 6 4 2

The Orion Publishing Group's policy is to use papers that are natural,
renewable ... ... made from wood grown in
sustainable forests. The logging and manufacturing processes ... expected
to conform to the environmental ... ... origin.

A catalogue record for this book is available from the British Library.

ISBN 978 1 4440 1027 5

Printed and bound in China

www.orionbooks.co.uk

To Lydia, Freya and Dominic,
with love

For my birthday
I was sent a little tree.

I dug a hole.

I planted it.

I watered it.

I tended it with care.

Summer came and went.

Autumn too.

Winter followed.

Then spring.

Then one morning I looked out
of the window.

There was my tree in all its glory.

Papa thought we should talk to his friend,
Mr Albert, about my little nut tree.

When we told him, Mr Albert
came to look for himself.

He asked if he might bring some gentlemen to look at my silver nutmeg and my golden pear.

They came straight away.

The news of my little nut tree
spread far and wide.
Everyone was talking
about me.

Everyone came to see
my little nut tree.

NUT
TREE
FOUND
HERE

NUT TREE GUIDES

Everyone came to see the silver
nutmeg and the golden pear.

Then one day a special letter
arrived.

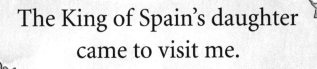

The King of Spain's daughter
came to visit me.

The princess walked into our house

and went straight to the nut tree.

The princess was horrid and wanted
to take it home with her.

The grand people told me
I could give no greater gift.

So I gave my little nut tree to the King of Spain's daughter.

Two footmen dug up my nut tree
and carried it away.

I felt very sad.
I felt it was unfair.

Then I saw the golden twig.

I flew on golden wings.

I skipped over water.

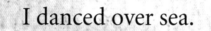

I danced over sea.

All the birds in the air

couldn't
catch me.

When I got home
I put my golden twig in a pot

and went upstairs to bed.

In the morning you wouldn't
believe what I saw!

Another little nut tree
– just for me!

Papa wrote a song about my nut tree.

I had a little nut tree
Nothing would it bear
But a silver nutmeg
And a golden pear

The King of Spain's daughter
Came to visit me
All for the sake
Of my little nut tree

I skipped over water
I danced over sea
All the birds in the air
Couldn't catch me

What are you going to read next?

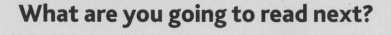

More adventures with

Horrid Henry,

or go
exploring
with

Shumba,

and brave the Jungle

and Arctic

with Algy.

Find a frog prince with Tulsa

or even a big, yellow, whiskery

Lion in the Meadow!

Tuck into some

Blood and Guts and
Rats' Tail Pizza,

learn to dance with

Sophie,

travel back
in time with

Cudweed

and sail away in

Noah's Ark.

Enjoy all the Early Readers.